DINOSAUR JUNIORS
Give Peas a Chance

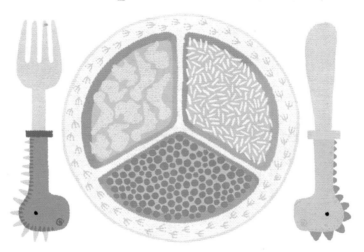

this book belongs to

....

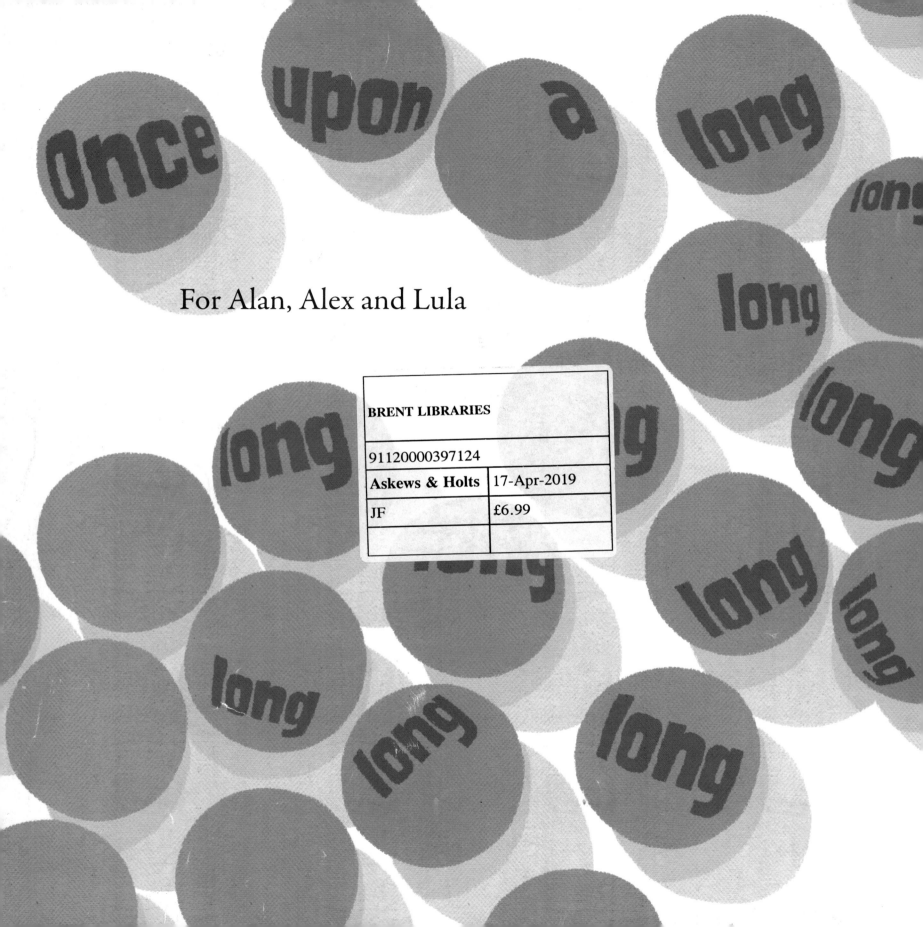

For Alan, Alex and Lula

DINOSAUR JUNIORS
Give Peas a Chance

Written and illustrated by

Rob Biddulph

HarperCollins *Children's Books*

First published in hardback in Great Britain by HarperCollins Children's Books in 2018
First published in paperback in 2019

HarperCollins Children's Books is a division of HarperCollins Publishers Ltd.
Text and illustrations copyright © Rob Biddulph 2018
The author / illustrator asserts the moral right to be identified as the
author / illustrator of the work. A CIP catalogue record for this book
is available from the British Library. All rights reserved.

Visit our website at www.harpercollins.co.uk

ISBN: 978-0-00-828063-5
Printed and bound in China
1 3 5 7 9 10 8 6 4 2

FIVE THINGS TO FIND IN THIS BOOK
1. A pea plant ☐
2. A green chameleon ☐
3. A clock showing 5pm ☐
4. Some broken sticks of chalk ☐
5. A rather fat toad ☐

Fun times! They're what life's all about.

A game.

A race.

A song.

GOAL!

A shout.

For one, the fun's about to stop...

TIME!

...shouts Nancy's pop.

"But, Dad, my friends..."

"Your friends can wait
Until I see an empty plate."

She sighs, and flops down in her seat.
Let's see what Nancy has to eat...

Ah. Dino Bites.
Well, they look nice.

And lovely, fluffy
dino rice.

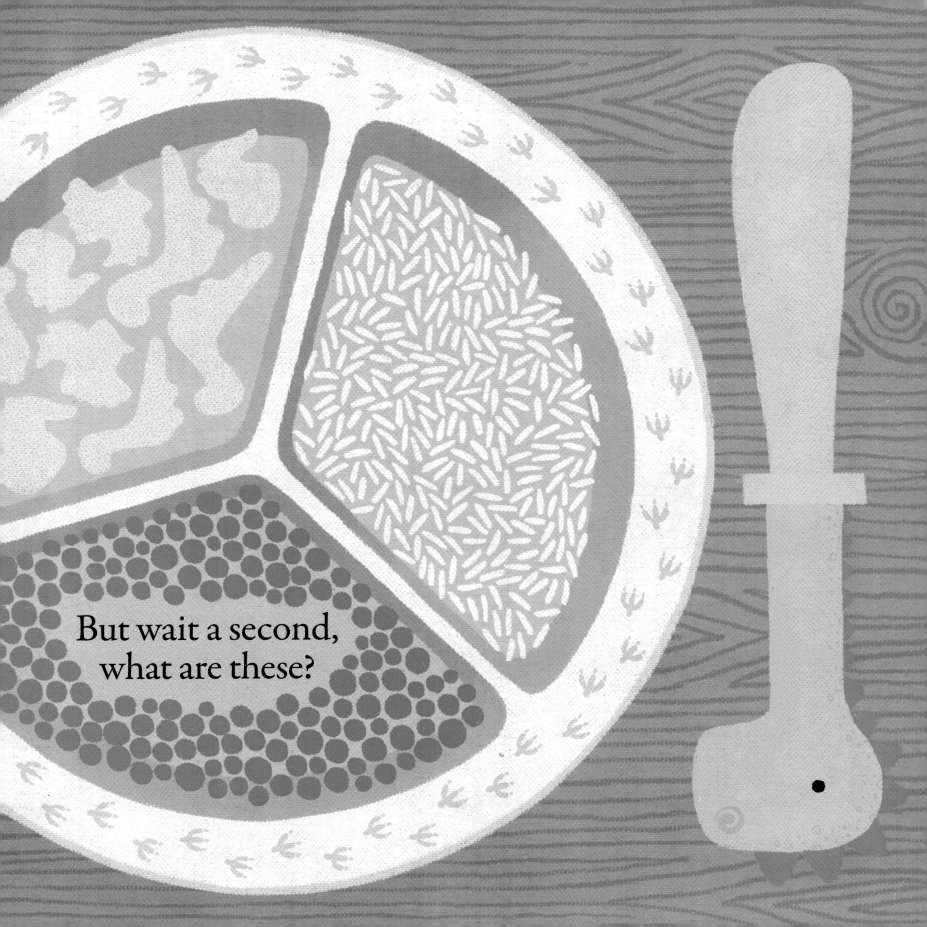

But wait a second,
what are these?

In truth, young Nancy isn't keen
On *any* food that's coloured green.
From leek to bean, she's not a fan.

But wait.
I think she has a plan...

Making sure that Greg can hear
She says it loud and says it clear:

"Mmmm, peas!
I'd eat them all day long.
Dad says they'll make me
super strong."

"Super strong?" thinks Greg. "Yes, please!
Then I could lift big rocks with ease
And build my tower really high...

...Hey, Nancy.
Can I have a try?"

"Ah, Greg. I didn't see you there.
Well maybe, just this once, I'll share.

Enjoy those peas.
I guarantee
They'll make you stronger.
Wait and see..."

Two minutes later, there goes Sue,
And Nancy knows just what to do:

"Mmmm, peas!
A treat from first to last.
Dad says they'll make me
super fast."

"Super fast?" thinks Sue. "How ace!
I'd never lose another race.
I want some peas. I really do...

...Hey, Nancy.
Can I have a few?"

"Ah, Sue. I didn't see you there.
Okay. I guess it's only fair.

Enjoy those peas.
I guarantee
They'll make you faster.
Wait and see..."

Finally, a game of chess.
What's Nancy plotting? Have a guess...

"Mmmm, peas!
A food to warm the heart.
Dad says they'll make me
super smart."

"Super smart?" thinks Otto. "Great!
At last, *my* chance to say 'checkmate'."
He tiptoes up, all smiley-faced...

"...Hey, Nancy.
Can I have a taste?"

"Ah, Otto. Didn't see you there.
Why, yes. I do have some to spare.

Enjoy those peas.
I guarantee
They'll make you smarter.
Wait and see..."

Nancy's plan has worked a treat.
There's nothing left for her to eat!

"I've finished, Dad! Is it okay
If I go back outside to play?"

Well, Dad is stunned. "Is this a trick?
I've never known you eat so quick!

My sweet, pea-loving dinosaur,
I've got good news...

...there's plenty more. "

Oh, Nancy! Look what's come about;
Your little plan has not worked out.

Enjoy those peas. I guarantee
They'll make you wiser...

...wait and see.